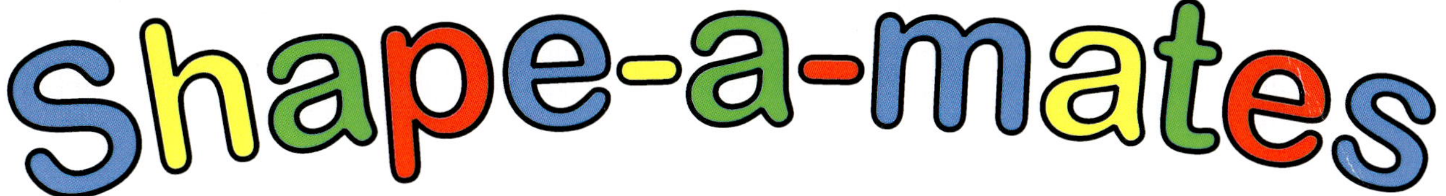

First published 2014 by
FASTPRINT PUBLISHING
Peterborough, England.

www.fast-print.net/store.php

SHAPE-A-MATES COLOURS AND SHAPES
Copyright © Marie Carter 2014
Illustrator - Brooke Carter

ISBN 978-178456-036-2

An environmentally friendly book printed and bound in England by
www.printondemand-worldwide.com

This book is made entirely of chain-of-custody materials

Hidden amongst the other trees in a forest far

away, grows a very special and magical tree

where the shape-a-mates live and play.

The shape tree is very special, it won't offer

you an apple or pear; instead it produces

different shapes all throughout the year.

Today it's sprouted four shapes: a triangle, a rectangle, a circle and a square.

Now let's go and meet the shape-a-mates and hear what information they have to share.

First here's Squeeze. He's picked the blue square to tell you all about, but you'll have to listen carefully because he doesn't like to shout.

A square has got four
corners and four sides
that all measure the
same; next time you see
one, try to remember
its name.

4

Next here's Circuit. She's chosen the yellow circle as it's
the one she likes the best. Let's listen as she tells us why
she prefers it to all the rest.

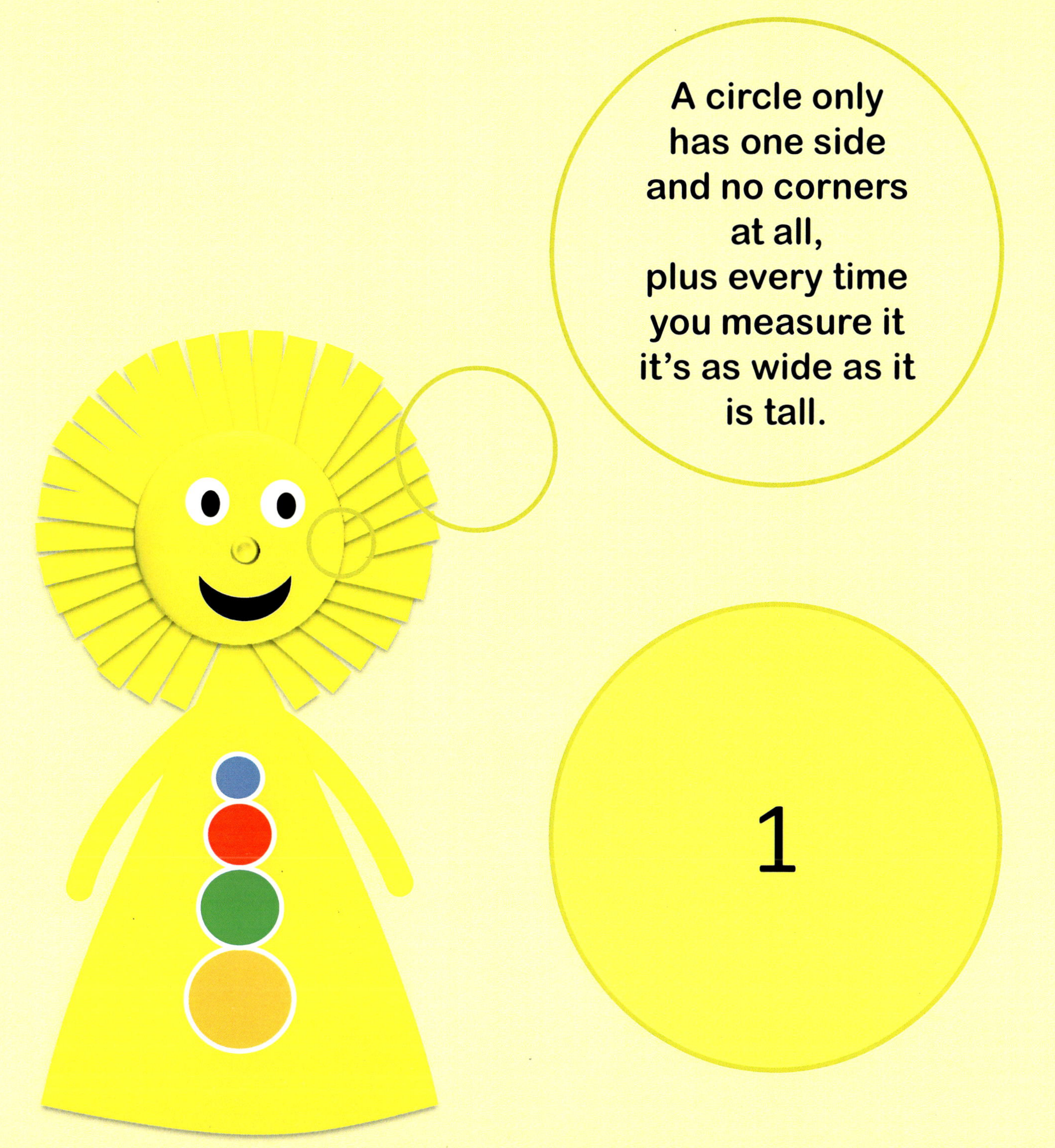

A circle only
has one side
and no corners
at all,
plus every time
you measure it
it's as wide as it
is tall.

1

Now here's Tizzy with the green triangle which he's holding very tight. When he's told you the number of corners and sides why don't you count to check he's right?

I've
counted
the corners
and the sides.
Both times I got to
three.
So now it's time to see if
I'm right!
Join in and count with
me.
1...2...3
3

Finally here's Rosie with the last shape off the tree;

it's called a rectangle and this one's red as you can see.

A rectangle has got four
sides, two long ones and
two short.
It also has four corners
but no curves of any sort.

Here are lots of other shapes the shape tree

might sometimes grow, take a good look at all

the colours, are there any you know?

Octagon
Star
Semi-circle
Pentagon
Heart
Diamond
Heptagon
Decagon
Hexagon
Nonagon

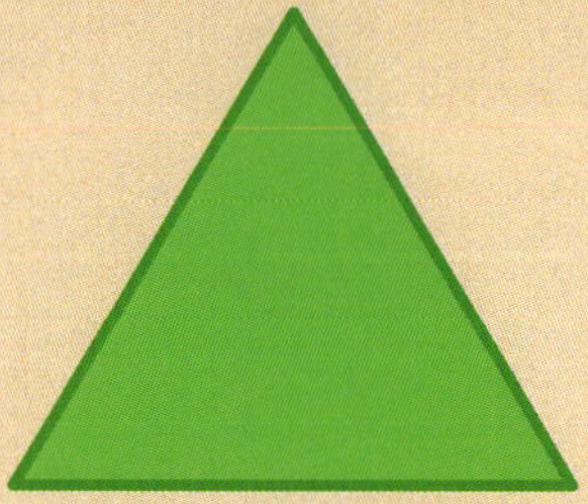

Now it's time to say goodbye, but remember to

keep looking all around, because there are

always lots of colours and shapes waiting to

be found.

1
2
3
4
4
5
6
7
8
9
10

shape-a-mates